COMING OF AGE 3: THE DAY OF SELF PLEASURE

ADULT FAIRY TALES
BOOK 15

VICTORIA RUSH

VOLUME 15

ADULT FAIRY TALES - BOOK 15

AUTHOR'S NOTE

All characters in this work of fiction are at least eighteen years of age.

COPYRIGHT

For the uninhibited...

1

———

When the three friends returned to their cabin after Tara's erotic performance on stage, they were still charged up and unable to sleep. Clover and Jessop hadn't anticipated Tara's exceptional contortion ability, and both of them were eager to try out her technique for themselves.

"That was *insane*, Tara!" Clover said, still feeling the insides of her thighs coated with lubrication from getting so turned on watching her.

"It was even sexier than when we tried sucking ourselves at the *erotic temple*," Jessop nodded. "This time you didn't need any help at all reaching your own pussy."

"Yeah," Tara blushed. "It took a bit of work and a fair amount of practice, but once I was able to get my feet behind my head, I was able to use my leg muscles to pull myself into position."

"You looked more like a *hedgehog* than a real person, curled up in that position," Clover chuckled.

"A very *sexy* hedgehog," Jessop nodded.

"I was worried you might hurt yourself, bending your spine that way," Clover said, pinching her eyebrows at Tara.

"It's not as bad as it looks," Tara laughed. "You just have to go slow and let your muscles stretch while you pull yourself closer..."

"Can you show us how to do it?" Jessop said. "I mean, that would be hot as hell being able to lick our own organs–"

"It might be easier for you than Clover," Tara nodded, glancing down at his hardening tool. "You've got an extra eight inch advantage over her, with your big erection."

"You're forgetting that I have a secret weapon of my *own*," Clover smiled, reaching into her satchel to retrieve the mage's magic crystals. "I can grow a dick of my own whenever I want to."

Tara glanced at the crystals, then peered up at Clover with a knowing grin.

"If you guys are up for it, I'm happy to show you how."

"Oh, I'm *up* for it alright," Clover grinned, rolling the crystals in the palm of her hand as they began to glow and hum softly.

"Okay," Tara said, noticing the bulb at the top of Clover's folds starting to grow and spread outward. "Let's begin by lying on the floor face-up with our legs pointed toward one another like a three-pointed star. That way, we can see what each other is doing and guide ourselves in the right direction."

"Not to mention watching each other's cocks and pussies to provide a little extra incentive," Jessop said, lifting his head a few inches after he lay down to glance at Clover's newly upstanding boy-cock and Tara's glistening pussy.

"Well, technically, there's only *one* pussy and two *cocks* in the mix now," Tara chuckled. "But this should work just fine the way it is." She paused for a moment as she peered at her two friends to make sure they were in the right position. "The first thing we need to do is swing our legs up in the air and slowly curl them down over your shoulders..."

"Like *this*?" Clover said, following Tara's instructions and placing the toes of her feet next to her head on the floor.

"Perfect," Tara said, staring at Clover's ballsack and her pointed erection aimed directly toward her face. "Now, wrap your arms around the underside of your knees and try walking your feet further upward while pulling your body into a more curled-up position..."

"I can feel it straining the back of my legs," Jessop grunted, awkwardly pulling his knees toward his head.

"It's going to feel a bit tight at first," Tara nodded as she walked her feet a few inches further away from her shoulders on the slick hardwood floor. "When you feel a little pain, pause for a moment to release the tension, then try to go another inch at a time."

"I can feel myself sliding from the sweat on my back," Clover said, wrinkling her forehead as she squinted at Tara between her legs. "I'm not sure how much this walking upside-down technique is stretching my body so much as just moving me closer toward you–"

"That's okay," Tara said, watching Jessop's and Clover's tilted hips slowly sliding closer toward hers. "Keep pushing until our butts touch together. Then we can use the counter-weight of our bodies to press against one another."

"Works for me," Jessop nodded when he felt his upturned ass press against Tara's.

"Mmm," Clover nodded when her cheeks melded against Tara's and Jessop's. "I can feel your juices sliding down your slit."

"And I can feel your balls caressing the crack of my ass," Tara grunted.

"This is much better," Jessop groaned as he flexed his feet on the floor to push his ass harder against each of his friends' backsides.

"Okay, now that we're locked in position," Tara nodded. "Try to pull your knees gently down toward your head. When they touch your shoulders, swing your feet around the back of your head, then interlock your ankles into a crossed position."

"Umfft," Jessop groaned while he stared at his dripping hard-on bobbing inches away from his flushing face. "It's a bit uncomfortable, but I sure like the view."

"No shit," Clover hissed, flexing her legs tighter as she pulled the tip of her ladyboy cock closer toward her mouth. "I always wondered what it would feel like to suck my own dick. I can almost taste it now..."

"Remember to go *slow*," Tara nodded, angling her dripping pussy closer toward her raised head as she watched her friends flicking the tip of their tongues inches away from their glistening crowns. "You don't want to hurt yourselves when you're so close to the prize. When you feel your muscles starting to pinch, pause for a moment and hold the position. Once you feel the tension beginning to ebb, try pushing an inch further."

"Oh my God," Jessop groaned as she swiped the tip of his glans with his outstretched tongue. "I can *touch* it now. I'm actually licking my own dick!"

"Mmm," Clover hummed as she pulled her flapping hard-on nearer to her lips. "I can taste my own pre-cum. Somehow, it doesn't taste as bad as when I'm going down on someone else."

"It's a singular pleasure, being able to suck your own sex," Tara nodded as she flicked the tip of her tongue over his tingling bead. "I suspect the delight in being able to lick yourself soon overrides any other thoughts or sensations you might have."

"You've got *that* right," Jessop shuddered when he felt the bulb of his glans slip between his lips. "This feels even better than when someone else does it to me."

"It's probably just the novelty of the experience," Tara grunted as she licked her throbbing clit while watching her friends sucking the tip of their reddening poles. "But you also know better than anyone else what you like and what feels best. Savor the pleasure while you bathe your dicks with your tongues..."

"Fuck me," Clover gasped when she was finally able to press her swelling crown into her waiting mouth. "Literally and figuratively. I'm actually *fucking* myself!"

"Don't try to talk now," Tara said, lifting her head for a moment while she smiled at her friends sucking their instruments as they flexed their bodies even further, pressing their erections further into their mouths. "Just enjoy the feeling while you focus on our bodies rocking together."

"Unghh," Jessop nodded, flaring his eyes while he watched Tara's dripping folds spreading open and Clover's instrument flexing in her mouth while they both sucked one another with red faces.

"Mhhhh," Clover groaned as she circled her tongue around the base of her helmet while she sucked the tip of her tool harder.

"Fuck, that's hot," Tara grunted, feeling their sweaty asses sliding together as they rocked their hips in unison, moaning in rising intensity.

When she saw both Clover and Jessop slide their mouths all the way down their poles to the base of their tightened balls, she couldn't hold it any longer. With a loud grunt, she sucked her clit hard into her pursed lips, then began spraying her juices all over her friends' shaking asses while she watched their shafts rhythmically pulsing and their eyes widening as they shot their loads deep down their own throats.

It seemed to take a lot longer than usual for each of the friends to stop shaking and convulsing as they moaned together in delirious, simultaneous pleasure, not wanting to miss a single pulse or squirt of their juices while they kept their faces locked against their quivering hips, darting their eyes from one person to the next until they finally finished shaking and groaning. When Clover and Jessop finally popped their dripping dicks out of their mouths, they peered up at one another with giant grins.

"So *that's* how you give a proper blow job," Clover smiled at Jessop.

"It's not so bad *swallowing* after all, is it?" Jessop nodded as his organ slapped against the front of his belly, leaving a trail of jism dripping up the front of his chest.

"I hardly even noticed, to be honest," Clover nodded. "I was so overcome with pleasure."

"You might want to try it in your *regular* state next time," Tara panted, still trying to catch her breath. "I suspect you'll find it just as intense when you're sucking your *little* bean as you do your larger one."

"I can't wait," Clover nodded as she stared at the stream of fluid dripping out of Tara's slit and down the crack of her ass.

"Maybe tomorrow," Tara sighed, pulling her legs back over her upturned body and resting them on top of each of her friend's heaving bellies. "I've had enough orgasms to last me a *week* at this point. Right now, I just need to sleep."

"Same here," Jessop said, following Tara's lead and

placing his outstretched legs softly over Clover's and Tara's stomachs while he closed his eyes languidly.

"You say that *now*," Clover chuckled, reaching out her left hand to hold Tara's right hand resting next to hers while she slipped the crystal balls into Tara's palm. "But you still haven't tried sucking yourself with a *cock*. I think we should see if these things work as well with *you* as they do with me."

"That's something to look forward to," Tara nodded, feeling herself losing consciousness while her friends' legs intertwined with her own as their bellies slowly rose and fell in approaching slumber.

2

The following day, the three friends kept themselves busy working in the fields while they mingled with some of the local natives. By now, they'd almost become accustomed to everyone walking around naked. Nobody paid much attention when a tribal girl bent over to plant seeds, even though her pussy was plainly exposed for everyone to see. But Clover noticed some of the younger men sporting hard-ons while they stole occasional glances at the women's figures, then they'd disappear into their cabins or the woods to quench their mounting desire.

It seemed an odd custom to force all the young people to wait until they were eighteen to express their sexual needs, when there was so much temptation literally staring them in the face every day. But Clover had to admit that the suppression of their natural coupling instinct gave them plenty of time to fantasize about more creative ways to satisfy their sexual curiosity. And it wasn't just the rest of the *tribe* that benefitted from their novel means of self-stimulation. Clover, Tara, and Jessop had also greatly expanded their erotic frame of reference in the process.

As dusk approached on the evening of the two-thirds moon, the trio were looking forward to another demonstration by one of the tribal youths, wondering what else he could possibly do to stimulate one straight-forward part of his anatomy. When they took their seats next to Gisella on the front row of the amphitheater, Clover gazed up at the starlit sky and smiled.

"How many more performances until the full moon?" she asked the old lady.

"Nine, including the one tonight."

"And we've got another *boy* presenting tonight?" Tara asked, squinting into the darkness behind the illuminated stage to get a glimpse of the next performer.

"Yes," Gisella nodded.

As the drummer began his usual drumbeat to announce the arrival of a new performer, Clover glimpsed at the empty stage with a wrinkled forehead.

"Any ideas what this one is going to bring to the table?" she said. "I don't see any props set up for him to use..."

"Sometimes the *simplest* way is the most erotic way," the old lady smiled. "I'm pretty sure you'll find his technique stimulating enough."

As another shadow approached the rear of the stage, the three friends squinted into the smoky fog, squeezing their legs together unconsciously in mounting curiosity. When the youth ascended the steps and walked out toward the center of the dais, he stopped in the middle of the candlelit stage, holding his hands behind his back.

"It looks like he's brought some kind of prop, after all," Jessop said, staring at the boy's lean, athletic build and the thick appendage hanging between his legs.

"I'm not sure he needs one," Tara said, grinding her thighs together while she soaked up the youth's figure. "I could get off just *staring* at that hot body all night."

"It's pretty sweet," Clover nodded, brushing her foot against Tara's on the stone floor of the stadium while playing with her friend's toes. "I'd be more than happy to give him his first *couples'* union if he and I were chosen winner at the end of the month."

Suddenly, the boy began to turn his body around in the flickering light of the surrounding candles, and when he had his back turned to the audience, everyone noticed that his hands were tightly tied together.

"How is he going to stimulate his cock in *that* condition?" Jessop said, shaking his head in dismay.

But by the time the youth turned around to face the crowd again, his organ had already lengthened to its fully erect state, standing proudly erect over his abdomen as it bounced softly over his navel.

"Maybe he's going to *lick* it with his tongue," Clover chuckled, reflecting back on the trio's erotic menage of the previous evening. "With a dick *that* size, I imagine it wouldn't be very difficult for him to reach it with his mouth."

While everybody admired his impressive organ and clapped softly, the youngster lowered himself into a squat position on the platform, then he slowly extended his legs in front of him, wiggling his toes playfully.

"Maybe he's just going to *tease* us all night long," Tara said as she slid her hand between Clover's quivering thighs.

While everybody in the audience became increasingly firm and wet wondering what the youth was planning to do, he slowly bent his right knee and slid the toes of his foot up he inside of his other thigh until they were pressing against his balls, fondling his testicles softly.

"Okay," Clover grinned, slipping her own hand between Tara's thighs to feel her rapidly moistening vulva. "There's something I haven't seen before."

"That's some pretty impressive flexibility," Tara nodded, tilting her hips upward to encourage Clover to press her hand deeper. "Can *you* do that, Jessop?"

"Not without a little help from my *hands*," Jessop grunted, pulling one of his feet awkwardly toward his crotch. "But I'm not sure what I'd do with only one foot if I got it that far, anyway."

As if on cue, the boy on the stage bent his other knee, then he pulled his other foot toward his upturned phallus, pressing the soles of both feet against the base of his pole.

"Ok," Jessop huffed, while trying to mimic the boy's technique. "There's no way I can bend myself that way–"

"He's probably had a bit more time to practice," Clover chuckled as she slipped one finger into Tara's dripping slit and pressed her thumb over her friend's throbbing clit.

"I'd practice with him *any* day," Tara moaned as she rocked her hips while she fingered Clover's pussy in kind.

Gisella peered at Jessop's inept attempt to stimulate himself with his feet while he toppled precariously beside her, then she smiled.

"Do you want some *help* with that?" she said, staring at his dripping head. "Your friends seem to have their hands busy elsewhere..."

"If you're offering," Jessop nodded, slipping his hand between Gisella's thighs and fingering her moist slit.

When the youth on the stage began to slide his feet up and down his bobbing shaft, a soft hum began to spread around the stadium while the rest of the crowd touched themselves in turn, groaning softly as they admired the pliability of the new performer. As he flexed his abdominal muscles trying to balance on his tightened ass, his mouth began to yawn open in rising pleasure while he tensed his leg muscles to squeeze his dick harder. But just as it seemed he was nearing climax from his rapidly pumping feet, he paused for a moment and pulled his feet away from his darkening cock, dripping rivulets of pre-cum down the sides of his shaft while it pulsed at the edge of a near-orgasm.

"What's he doing now?" Clover said, furrowing her brow at the brink of her own climax while Tara fingered her pussy enthusiastically. "Just when I was about to come along with him–"

"I don't know," Tara panted while Clover pressed her fingers deep into her throbbing cunt. "But something tells me he's going to finish another way..."

As the boy lifted his left foot higher toward the top of his dripping erection, he flexed the big toe and his long toe slightly apart, gripping his dripping crown tightly between the two digits. Then he lowered the toes of his other foot beneath his balls and inserted the other big toe directly into his ass.

"Holy fuck!" Jessop grunted as Gisella stroked his cock with both hands and he trilled her hardening nub at the same time. "How is he able to do that?"

"I don't know," Clover said, placing her hand atop Tara's to press her harder against her burning gland while she jerked her other hand inside her friend's sopping pussy. "But something tells me he's practiced this technique a few times before."

"Do you want a little stimulation of your *own* down there?" Gisella said, glancing at Jessop's flushed face.

"With your *toe*?" he said, furrowing his brow as he peered down at her parted thighs. "That might be a little difficult in our present configuration."

"Not to worry," the old lady smiled, lowering one hand below his tightening testicles and inserting two fingers deep into his flexing sphincter. "I have a little experience in this area. I happen to know just where you boys like to be stimulated..."

As she curled her fingers upward to massage Jessop's prostate gland, Jessop tilted his head upward, groaning loudly. Meanwhile, the youth on the stage had begun flexing his right leg, jamming his toe harder against his throbbing internal organ while he jerked his other foot over his dripping hard-on while he gripping the glans tightly between the two toes of his other foot. Within seconds, his dick began spurting long ropes of thick white cum high into the air above his shaking body, and the rest of the audience groaned in tandem as everyone climaxed hard while they stimulated themselves and their adjacent partners.

After the group on the front steps of the stadium had finished squirting and jetting their own juices over one another, they retracted their hands from between each other's legs, glancing at one another's flushed faces.

"Just when I thought it couldn't get any weirder or kinkier," Clover panted, sliding her slippery hand over Tara's erect nipples.

"Or more twisted and contorted," Tara said, still holding her dripping hand over Clover's burning pussy.

"It looks like we're going to have to up our game," Jessop nodded as he rubbed his creamy cum over the tip of his swelling crown. "If one of us is going to have a chance at joining the couples' demonstration at the end of the month."

"I'm way ahead of you," Clover said, smiling at the old

lady. "There's only *one* of us left to impress the judges. And I'm already thinking of new ways to bend my body in ways none of them have imagined..."

3

fter the show, the three friends returned to their cabin and flopped onto the bed, exploring new ways to stimulate one another with only their toes. Although they ended up laughing more often than moaning in pleasure from their clumsy probing, it was a fun way to wind down from another exotic stage performance and they all fell asleep satisfied and happy. In the morning, they talked a bit further about what Clover could do to impress the judges with her own presentation, and after trying out some new combinations, they returned to the amphitheater for another group supper before sitting down for a new performance.

"I'm excited to see what our next presenter will bring to the table," Clover said, snuggling up next to Gisella on the front steps of the arena.

"Do you *prefer* watching girls, or are you more intrigued discovering new ways to stimulate yourself?" the old lady said, glancing down at her shaved pussy.

"A little bit of both," Clover smiled. 'Although I also appreciate a few *hard* things when the mood strikes me."

"Well, it looks like you've got a convenient one to play with whenever you want," Gisella chuckled, peering at Jessop's lengthening tool as he caressed the insides of Tara's thighs. "Have the three of you been trying out some of the new techniques you've seen demonstrated on the stage?"

"A few," Clover nodded. "Some more successfully than others. But Jessop's isn't the *only* cock I've had fun practicing with."

"I bet," Gisella said, sliding her fingers slowly over the front of Clover's mound. "With a figure like yours, I imagine you have no shortage of gentlemen callers."

"And *women*," Clover groaned when Gisella slipped her hand between her thighs, massaging her pearl gently with her fingers. "Sometimes a woman's soft body is just as pleasurable to rub against as a man's hard parts."

"Well, I suspect you'll find tonight's performer has *plenty* of soft parts to rub against," Gisella nodded as she squinted into the smoky fog lingering behind the stage.

As the drumbeat began to announce the arrival of a new presenter to the stage, the three friends peered through the flickering candles, noticing another naked tribal girl walking toward the central ring. When she ascended the steps and stopped in the middle of the dais, she stood with her legs slightly parted and her hands clasped softly behind her back.

"Mmm," Clover panted, rolling her hips gently on the cold marble step while Gisella teased her pussy. "I like it when the performers surprise us with their little secrets."

While the audience applauded to acknowledge the girl's courage in presenting herself to the crowd, she smiled demurely, moving one hand slowly behind her back. Suddenly, a white feather poked out between her parted egs as she caressed it over her glistening vulva. As she rocked her hips gently, she moaned, closing her eyes.

"Ohhh..." Clover groaned while Gisella flitted her fingertips over her swelling labia.

"You *like*?" the old lady smiled, watching Clover's teats slowly harden and swell.

"I like," Clover grunted, rocking her hips harder to encourage Gisella to rub her pussy harder.

"Sometimes the softest touch is the most erotic," Gisella nodded, pinching her fingers together as she slid them slowly over the sides of Clover's folds.

"Yes," Clover shuddered, unable to take her eyes off the girl's gyrating hips while she swiped the feather back and forth over her moistening vulva from behind.

Suddenly, the girl pulled the feather from between her legs and raised it to her face, sliding it under her nose while she breathed in the scent of her own juices.

"Do you like the smell of a woman's sex?" Gisella said, lifting her dripping fingers to her face and spreading Clover's nectar over her lips.

"Yes, and the *taste*," Clover grunted, squeezing her thighs harder together while trying to stimulate her throbbing bean.

"Indeed," the old lady grinned, running the tip of her tongue sensuously over her upper lip. "There's nothing quite so satisfying as the flavor of a woman's pleasure."

When the girl on the stage began to gently lower the feather, sliding the tip over her upturned chin and down the front of her neck, Gisella did the same with the back of her hand, mimicking the movement of the feather.

"Unghh," Clover groaned, tilting her tits upward to meet Gisella's lowering fingers.

The girl continued sliding the feather between the cleft

of her cleavage and over the tips of her pointed teats with Gisella matching her movements, barely touching Clover's skin with the tips of her fingers as she circled Clover's puckering areolas and rising goosebumps over her tingling flesh.

"That feels so good–" Clover panted, heaving her chest in rising pleasure from the old lady's ministrations.

"This young lady knows what the rest of us have known for a long time," Gisella nodded, pinching Clover's teats between her middle fingers and her adjacent forefinger as she rolled them softly in her hands. "That a long, slow buildup is the best part of any erotic performance."

"Yes," Clover grunted as she rolled her hips on the warm step next to Gisella. "And the part that makes the *ending* all the more satisfying."

"So it would seem," the old lady laughed, noticing the thick puddle forming on the step between Clover's parted legs. "The longer the foreplay, the stronger the climax."

"Touch my pussy," Clover panted, spreading her legs further apart as she begged Gisella to move her hands lower. "You're driving me crazy–"

"That's the idea," Gisella smiled, squeezing Clover's breasts while she pinched her nipples harder. "The longer you wait, the happier you'll be when we finally get there."

As the girl on the stage began sliding the feather down the front of her quivering abdomen, Clover could feel herself trembling in sympathy, groaning softly when the girl paused over her thick bush, sliding the tines of the feather between her soft curls.

"Do you prefer the touch of *smooth* skin?" Gisella said, sliding her hand further down Clover's stomach, over her bare mound.

"Sometimes," Clover nodded, feeling her juices trickling down her slit and between the crack of her ass. "But I also like the feel of a girl's moist bush when I'm kissing her down there–"

"Would you like *me* to kiss you down there?" Gisella said, pausing the movement of her hand above her tingling gland.

"Yes, please," Clover grunted, rotating her hips on the dripping step while she watched the girl stroking her muff like a bow on a Stradivarius.

Gisella turned her body, then she knelt down in front of Clover's knees, slowly parting her legs and pressing her face next to Clover's steaming pussy. When her lips almost touched her tingling vulva, she paused just short, blowing gently on Clover's petals while a river of juices streamed down between her slit.

"Mffft," Clover grunted, trying unsuccessfully to press her pussy into the old lady's face.

But when the girl on the stage finally lowered the spine of her feather and began sliding it over her glistening vulva, Gisella reached out her tongue and swiped it slowly up the length of Clover's cleft like a puppy licking its owner's face.

"Yes," Clover huffed, placing her hands impatiently over the back of Gisella's head. "Suck my pussy. Lick my cunt and make me come in your mouth. I need this so bad–"

"Uh-uh," the old lady murmured, pulling her face back slightly as she glanced at Clover's spreading lips and the fountain of juices streaming down her gash. "Not until the girl on the stage is ready..."

Clover lifted her head and gazed at the girl on the platform, noticing her moving her hips rhythmically as she swiped the feather faster between her legs, tilting her head upward in escalating pleasure.

"It looks like she's getting close..." Clover said, glancing down at Gisella with pleading eyes. "I think we're *both* ready–"

Gisella turned her head to peer at the girl on the stage, noticing her legs starting to tremble and a deep flush beginning to spread over her quivering breasts, then she buried her face back between Clover's thighs, flicking her tongue over her burning bulb as she slid the fingers of one hand between Clover's crack. When she felt Clover slowly tilting her hips upward while she tensed her buttock muscles over her hand, the old lady slipped her thumb into Clover's hole, rolling it gently over her G-spot while she sucked Clover's gland hard into her mouth.

When the girl on the stage began grunting in climactic pleasure and jerking her body in convulsive spasms while she held the feather between her quivering legs, Clover couldn't hold it any longer, squirting her juices all over Gisella's face while they groaned together in simultaneous pleasure. Clover had been so focused on her own pleasure and that of the girl's on the stage that she hadn't paid any attention to her two other friends, who were groaning along with the rest of the audience in ecstasy while Tara rocked her hips over Jessop's hard-on, riding him in the reverse cowgirl position. When everybody finally finished shaking and squirting, Gisella pulled her face away from Clover's dripping thighs, peering up at her with a satisfied smile.

"Sorry about that," Clover said, swiping a few loose, wet strands away from the side of Gisella's face. "I guess I got a little carried away by the girl's performance. That might have been the hottest one I've seen yet."

"I'm glad you enjoyed it," the old lady nodded, wiping Clover's juices off the side of her cheek with the back of her hand. "Sometimes the greatest pleasure comes from the softest of touches."

Clover glanced between Gisella's legs, noticing her juices still streaming down the insides of her thighs.

"What about *you*?" she said, pinching her eyebrows together. "Do you need a little stimulation of your own to finish the job? It looks like we were the ones having most of the fun here–"

"Don't worry about me," Gisella grinned. "I climaxed just as hard as you when I felt you squirting your love juices. I enjoyed my own long, slow buildup from my front-row seat of *another* sexy girl's performance."

4

That night, Clover, Tara, and Jessop took a break from experimenting in their own cabin, having already climaxed four times in the previous two days. The following day, the three friends spent some extra time helping the tribespeople working in the fields while they sized up the youths that had already performed on the stage and those still waiting to do so. They knew each of them might have a chance at being chosen to be one of the winners for the couple's demonstration, and while they planted seeds and harvested the vegetables from the plantation, they fantasized about what they would do if they had a chance to hookup with one of the sexy natives.

Clover knew it was the boys' turn to put on another demonstration tonight, and while she leaned over the tilled soil, displaying her shaved pussy for all the young people to gaze at, her vulva glistened in anticipation of another erotic performance. She knew that if she were chosen to perform at the end of the month, she would likely transform into her ladyboy guise, and she was torn between wanting a boy or a girl to match up with. On the one hand, she thought, if it vere a boy, she could enjoy his big cock before she turned nto a shemale, but if it were a girl, she'd be able to give the youngster a ride she'd never even dreamed of.

So many choices, Clover grinned as she ogled the naked figures of the youths working in the field. who were pretending not to stare at the three strangers and their glistening, white bodies.

When dusk fell over the village and it came time for the evening's performance, Clover was already dripping in anticipation, choosing to sit next to Jessop so she could watch his reaction to the boy's new self-stimulation technique. Half of the fun of watching every performance was seeing the reaction of the crowd to the youths' erotic presentations, including that of her friends and also Gisella, each of whom seemed to get turned on as much as she did. The old lady had surprised her with her enthusiastic response to the young peoples' auto-erotic demonstrations, which only served to reinforce how their unique custom of having every youth masturbate in public kept everyone's sex lives vibrant and interesting.

"Are you looking forward to watching a new *boy* perform tonight?" Clover said, rubbing the side of her thigh teasingly against Jessop's sweaty leg.

"Always," he nodded, caressing the tip of his tingling organ in anticipation of another exciting performance.

"Which do you enjoy more?" Clover said. "Imagining yourself *hooking up* with them, or looking forward to trying out some of their new techniques when you're all alone?"

"That's a tough one," Jessop grinned. "I've certainly enjoyed trying some of their novel methods, but I have to admit that I wouldn't mind sucking or stroking some of those beautiful brown hard-ons if I had a chance..."

"Maybe Gisella will allow us to mingle with the group

more openly after we've each had our turn on the stage,
Clover nodded. "It seems as if they're free to couple up
however they please once they popped their cherry, in a
manner of speaking."

"Let's hope so," Jessop grunted as his dick began to rise
between his legs when he heard the familiar drumbeat
announcing the arrival of a new performer to the stage.

The two friends glanced at the stage, noticing a small
wooden stool arranged at knee height in the middle of the
illuminated dais, squinting their eyes.

"What do you think he's going to do with that?" Jessop
said, grasping his dick tightly when it bounced against his
stomach.

"I don't know," Clover said, reaching down to squeeze his
balls while his glans twitched instinctively. "But something
tells me he's not just going to *sit* on it."

As another lean youth emerged from the darkness
behind the stage and ascended the steps to walk out to the
middle of the platform, they ran their eyes over his
muscular and lithe figure while they trilled their private
parts absentmindedly.

"He's pretty hot," Clover nodded as she slid a finger up
the crease of her dripping pussy. "Would you suck *that* boy's
cock if you had a chance?"

"I have to wait to see what it looks like when it's angry,"
Jessop grinned as a dribble of precum oozed out the tip of
his erection.

The boy on the stage paused for a moment while he
listened to the applause of the crowd, then he walked over
toward the side of the stage, picking up one of the tall
candles flickering around the perimeter and placed it
upright on the middle of the empty stool.

"What is he going to do with that?" Clover said, pinching her eyebrows together in curiosity.

"I'm not sure," Jessop panted as he rolled his thumb over his slippery crown. "But whatever it is, it seems to already be having the desired effect."

As the youth's flaccid penis slowly began to rise and swell in front of the flickering candle, he stepped forward a couple of paces, placing his hips and his balls a few inches over the flame.

"What the–?" Jessop said, flaring his eyes open while he stopped the movement of his hand over his throbbing dick. "That doesn't look very safe *or* stimulating."

"Tell that to the *boy*," Clover said, sliding her fingers over her tingling clit while she stared at the sexy youth, mesmerized by what he would do next. "Judging by the reaction of his cock, he seems to be finding it very stimulating."

The youth held his position over the flame until his phallus has risen to its full upright position, casting a long shadow over the floor of the stage next to the stool. Then he pulled back for a moment, parting his mouth open in pleasure while his hard-on bobbed excitedly over his stomach.

"What about now?" Clover said, sliding the finger of one hand up the underside of Jessop's flapping erection. "Would you suck him *now*?"

"Fuck, yes," Jessop grunted, grabbing his dick with both hands and pumping it excitedly. "I'd suck, stroke, or frot that thing, any day–"

"Even if it were positioned over the flame?" Clover grinned.

"It might be kind of fun," Jessop nodded. "I've never tried that before."

While everybody stared at the sexy youth, admiring his thick instrument, the boy slowly pressed his hips forward again, this time moving the tip of his cock directly over the top of the flickering candle. It seemed from their perspective that it was only a couple of inches from the searing flame, and Clover and Jessop wondered how he could stand to keep it so close to the heat source for so long.

"He's going to *burn* it if he keeps it there much longer," Clover said, wrinkling her forehead in concern.

"I'm pretty sure he's tested this a few times before," Gisella chuckled, sitting next to Tara on their opposite side. "I imagine he knows what he's doing."

"Look how *red* it's getting," Tara said, tilting her body forward while she stared at the boy's cock.

"That's one of the benefits of extra heat," the old lady nodded. "It promotes blood circulation to the affected area and also causes increased swelling..."

"It seems to be working," Jessop said as he gazed at the boy's thickening glans. "If he keeps it under the flame much longer, that thing is going to *explode*."

As if on cue, the youth on the stage pulled his pole slowly away from the flame and tilted his hips upward to display the underside of his erection for the rest of the crowd. While it pulsed and bounced over his hips, his testicles nestled up tightly against the base of his cock, looking like two robins' eggs in a nest.

"It looks like he's getting ready to explode for an entirely *different* reason," Clover panted, slipping two fingers into her throbbing cavity as she dribbled her juices over her butt cheeks.

"Who knew that placing your dick over a flame could be so exciting?" Tara nodded as she and Gisella gently fingered each other's pussies.

"Yes, but is it going to be enough to put him over the *edge*?" Jessop said, fapping his dick harder while he admired the youth's carved body in the shadow of the flickering candle.

"Maybe not," Clover said as she watched the boy lift the candle off the stool and tilt it sideways over his throbbing organ. "I think he has other plans for this candle..."

The youth positioned the tip of the candle over the base of his cock, then he paused as a drop of hot wax fell onto his shaft. His dick flexed upward immediately, emitting a drop of precum out of the tip of his pole while he moaned softly.

"Fuck, that's hot," Tara grunted, rolling her hand more vigorously between Gisella's parted legs while the old lady returned the favor.

"In more ways than one," Clover said, parting her mouth open in shock while she stared at the youth's bobbing phallus.

"I have got to try me some of that," Jessop nodded, stroking his dick harder as streams of cum slid down the sides of his upturned erection.

"You might want to wait until he *finishes* his demonstration," Clover chuckled. "Like they say on those reality shows back home, you shouldn't necessarily try this at home."

"Yeah, well I'm sure as fuck enjoying *this* reality show," Jessop groaned as his own swelling glans began to darken in rising pleasure.

While the rest of the crowd peered on, mesmerized by the boy's unusual self-stimulation technique, the youth shifted the candle further along the length of his bobbing hard-on, gently tilting it up and down as successive drops of hot wax splattered over his purple phallus. Each time the wax dropped closer toward his swelling crown, another drop of pre-cum drizzled out the tip, creating a waterfall of glistening strings falling toward the floor. As he moved the tip of the candle directly over his glistening corona, his dick bounced upward a few times, as if pleading for him to finish his erotic demonstration. He glanced up at the audience, and when he dripped the final wad of hot wax over his flexing pole, he groaned loudly, ejecting a series of long ropes over the top of the stool, shooting all the way to the base of the grandstand.

"Whoa!" Clover gasped, shifting her body to the side to avoid the jet of splooge.

But Jessop had the opposite reaction, turning his body in the direction of the shooting semen, coating his dick with the slippery liquid as he shot his own powerful load outward in the opposite direction. While the youth on the stage stood ramrod straight on the stage, watching his dick jetting one long string of cum after another in multiple directions toward the crowd, they groaned along with him, stroking and jilling themselves in unison while they gaped their mouths open in simultaneous pleasure.

"Oh my God," Tara panted next to Gisella as the two women jerked their bodies with their hands planted between each other's thighs. "Just when I thought it couldn't get any weirder...or hotter."

"It was pretty *hot* alright," Clover shuddered, pulling her fingers out of her dripping hole while she peered at the youth's dick bouncing slower as it stopped emitting cum and began to soften, dangling down over his dripping thigh. "That's one technique we've definitely got to try when we get our first chance."

"Do you mind if we take some of those candles back to our cabin?" Tara said, grinning at the old lady as she slid her hand from the inside of her slippery thigh.

"Have at it," Gisella smiled. "I might even take one or two for my *own* personal pleasure."

"Would you care to join us?" Clover said, lifting one eyebrow.

"I don't know," Gisella said, wrinkling her forehead. 'Don't you think that will make things a little unbalanced in your cabin with three pussies and only one cock to play with?"

"We might be able to rectify that quickly enough," Clover grinned at Gisella. "We've been keeping a few surprises of our own while we await our final turn on the stage."

"I can't wait to see," the old lady nodded. "I'll be happy to join you to test out some of your new self-stimulation strategies..."

5

___

When the foursome returned to the visitors' cabin, they arranged some candles then fell onto the bed and rubbed their bodies together while they relived the sexy performance of the boy on the stage. Everybody wanted a turn with Gisella, who turned out to be surprisingly firm and flexible for a woman of her age. She had large brown eyes, plump full lips, and a figure that defied her years. Although her breasts sagged slightly, they were still round and firm, with long nipples protruding from her saucer-sized medallions. And her ass, though somewhat larger than some of the younger tribeswomen, was smooth and muscular, reflecting her many years of labor bending over in the field. But her most interesting feature was her vulva, which had much larger and puffier labia than other women, with a prominent bulge at the apex of her folds, where her clitoris nestled like a cherry tomato.

"God, you're beautiful," Clover said while she kissed the insides of Gisella's thighs as Tara and Jessop worshipped the other parts of her body in their own way. "I've been so busy admiring the figures of the sexy young people on the stage, I barely noticed we had another vixen hiding in plain sight."

"You were a little distracted by what they were doing," Gisella chuckled. "So I guess I can excuse your oversight."

"As were *you*," Clover nodded, moving her head a little higher while she sucked Gisella's swollen labia into her mouth. "I'm happy to see that you and the rest of the elders seem to enjoy the erotic performances as much as we do."

"Why wouldn't we?" Gisella grinned. "Our sex drive is just as strong as it was when we were younger, and the new techniques displayed by the youngsters gives us lots of new material to keep us active and engaged."

"Alone, or as *partners*?" Clover asked.

"With whomever we please," Gisella smiled. "And in whatever combinations we enjoy."

"You mean in combinations of more than *two*?" Clover said, tilting her eyebrows.

"Of course," the old lady smiled. "The more the merrier."

"Well, there's *four* of us now," Clover said, peering up at her friends, who were sucking Gisella's breasts while she rocked her hips against Clover's face. "How would you like to hook up with us all together this time?"

"Hmm," Gisella said, glancing at Jessop's hard-on as he circled the tip of it over her hard teats. "I'd love to suck your boy's big poker, but that will leave three pussies unattended..."

"Not necessarily," Clover smiled, reaching over to her satchel and pulling out the mage's magic crystals while rolling them in her hand. "I told you we had we had something special we've been hiding–"

While the balls began to glow and hum in her palm, Clover spread her legs apart as Gisella's eyes widened watching her clitoris slowly swell and push out until she was sporting a thick, throbbing erection bobbing over her stomach.

"That's something special indeed," the old lady said, leaning forward to inhale Clover's tool while she bathed her tongue around the underside of her sensitive frenulum.

"Hey!" Jessop grunted. "I thought *I* was going to be the lucky recipient of your expert fellatio?"

"Okay," Gisella said, pulling her head off Clover's bobbing pole and glancing at Jessop's dripping organ. "We might be able to find another way to keep each of us engaged..."

"What did you have in mind?" Clover said. "Now that we have *two* cocks and two pussies to work with?"

Gisella paused while she peered at each of the three friends and their glistening sexes, then she nodded slowly.

"How about if you lie down on the bed face up while I straddle you, facing your feet? Then, while you probe my yoni with your impressive instrument, Tara can sit in front of me while we rub our tits and pussies together."

"Where do I fit into the equation?" Jessop said, twisting his forehead into a disappointed frown.

"You can stand with your dick at face height, while Tara and I suck and lick it together."

"Fuck, yes," Jessop grunted while his dick flexed excitedly upward, nodding in agreement.

"Shall we assume the positions then?" Gisella said, grinning at Clover.

"You don't have to ask twice," Clover nodded, lying face-up with her dick flapping over her belly.

Gisella parted her legs while she squatted over Clover's midsection, pointing the tip of her tool toward her dripping opening, then she slowly lowered her hips over Clover's throbbing hard-on while the two women moaned in pleasure. When Tara saw Gisella's clit beginning to push out of her hood and extending outward like a little cock of its own, she wasted no time kneeling in front of the old lady as she pressed her hips and breasts hard against her stomach.

"Ungnn," Tara groaned when she felt Gisella's nub slide over her tingling bulb. "You're so hot–"

"Hot, sexy?" Gisella grunted with the two girls while they rocked their hips together. "Or hot as in warm body?"

"Both," Tara said, tilting her head forward to thrust her tongue into Gisella's mouth as they began to kiss passionately.

"The view from back here isn't so bad either," Clover nodded, reaching her hands forward to clasp the side of Gisella's ass while she rocked her hips over Clover's dick and ground her pussy against Tara's.

"Nor *here*," Jessop shuddered, rolling his dick against the sides of Tara's and Gisella's faces while they kissed and moaned in each other's mouths.

When he slapped his dick softly against the sides of their cheeks, they pulled back for a moment and yawned their mouths open while Jessop pressed his tool between their lips as they flicked their tongues over his dripping crown.

"Damn," Jessop groaned as he ran the fingers of both hands through the women's long, flowing hair. "Now *there's* a performance I haven't seen for a while–"

"And it's three times as good," Clover said as she watched the head of Jessop's erection popping in and out the side's of the women's heads while she pumped her ladyboy cock deep into Gisella's hole and the two women's combined juices poured down between her crack.

"This is way too fucking sexy," Jessop hissed, clenching his teeth together as he tried to make the exquisite feeling of his two-way blowjob last. "I'm not going to be able to hold out much longer..."

"Yes, baby," Gisella nodded, tilting her head to one side while she flicked her tongue under the fleshy side of Jessop's corona. "Let it rip while I feel Clover jet her spunk in my pussy. I want to feel Tara gushing her juices all over my throbbing button."

"Muhhh," Tara moaned as she tilted her head in the opposite direction to suck Jessop's tightening balls. "I'm going to come with you, Jessop. I want to feel you pulse in my mouth when I squirt..."

Suddenly, all four of the lovers grunted loudly as their combined bodies began to shake and squirt while they rocked their bodies in unison, gripping each other tightly. Every one of them had a front-row seat as they peered at each other's faces gaping in pleasure and flushing in climax while their bodies jerked and throbbed in ecstasy. When they finally finished coming together, Jessop dropped to his knees, sliding his dripping tool between Tara's and Gisella's slippery abdomens while Clover savored the sensation of their combined juices dripping over her throbbing slit and under her glistening ass.

"That took long enough," Clover panted as she pinched Gisella's ass from behind.

"What, for each of us to climax this time?" the old lady said, pinching her eyebrows together.

"No," Clover smiled. "To finally get you in the sack with all three of us. It was fun playing with you separately while we watched the shows on the stage, but nowhere near as exciting as having you all for ourselves at the same time."

"Well, pretty soon you'll have *lots* of opportunity to hook up with whomever you wish," Gisella nodded. "There's only one more of you waiting for a turn on the stage, and with his little extra twist thrown into the mix, I'm pretty sure Clover's got a good shot at joining the couples' demonstration in a few more days."

"It's not just a *couple* I plan to show my skills with," Clover grinned, pulling her dick out of Gisella's hole and slapping it playfully against the old lady's dripping bush. "Now that I've got both a cock and a pussy to play with, I plan on hooking up with every one of those sexy tribal youths, and not necessarily one at a time."

"You and me, *both*," Gisella chuckled as she gripped Clover's tool tightly, squeezing the last drops of cum out of the tip. "I'm tired of sitting on the sidelines letting the youngsters have all the fun."

6

———

After seeing how Clover could transform into a shemale, Gisella quickly scheduled her to be the final performer of the month before the full moon, anticipated to arrive in five days. She didn't want to deny the audience an opportunity to witness her unique skills for themselves, plus she was eager to see what the girl from the far side of the world would surprise her with next.

The three friends slept well that night, and upon returning to the amphitheater the following day, they competed to see who would sit next to the old lady. She had surprised them with her willingness to try anything, and she'd proven herself adept at using every part of her body to please both her male and female partners. When Jessop squeezed in next to her on the right side and Tara took the open seat to her left, Clover peered at the old lady with a knowing grin.

"It appears you've become the top draw at tonight's performance," she chuckled, noticing Tara's and Jessop's legs widening while Gisella caressed the insides of their thighs.

"Hardly," Gisella said, watching Jessop's organ thickening and pressing against the side of his leg. "But I'll be happy to keep your friends amused while they take in another show."

"Like you did last night?" Clover smiled.

"We might have to be a little more *discreet* this time so as not to distract from the display on the stage," Gisella nodded.

"Speaking of," Clover said, watching two burly tribesmen lift a large object covered with a cloth tarp onto the middle of the platform. "We've got a *girl* performing tonight, right?"

"Yes," Gisella said. "And judging by the size of that concealed prop, it promises to be quite interesting."

As the drummer began his drumbeat to announce the arrival of the next performer to the stage, Clover scanned the cloaked object, trying to discern its purpose. It appeared to be about the size of a normal person, sitting in a squat position with its back facing the crowd. It was hard to tell if it was in the form of a man or a woman, and as she squinted at the form's cross-legged posture, her pussy began to moisten, reflecting back on the previous night's hookup. She was hoping to see more girl-on-boy simulations, and as the shadow of another naked girl approached the back of the stage, her clit tingled in anticipation of seeing another unexpected performance.

After the girl ascended the steps, she walked out toward the center of the dais, standing beside the concealed form while the audience applauded softly. When the clapping died down, she reached one hand up to the top of the cloak, then she pulled the cover off the form, tossing it to the side of the stage. It was a large wooden block, carved in the shape of a man's body with his arms straightened behind his back to support the weight of his body. The effigy looked super-realistic, with sinewy muscles rippling almost like a mini statue of David. Whoever had carved it had obviously spent a great deal of time getting every detail perfected and anatomically correct.

But when the girl grasped the form with two hands and slowly began to turn it around to present the other side to the crowd, a faint gasp arose from the audience. The face and form of the sculpture matched the image of Jessop almost exactly, right down to the size and shape of his upturned erection, standing proudly upright in his lap, polished and sanded to a perfect reproduction.

"Holy shit!" Clover grunted, elbowing Jessop in the side as he trembled in shock next to her. "It seems that you have a secret admirer."

"A very *talented* admirer," Tara nodded, squinting her eyes at the detail of the carving.

"I'm just glad she carved my *dick* correctly," Jessop chuckled, as his cock rose quickly between his legs, matching the form of the bust. "I'm surprised she remembered what it looks like when it isn't covered in bees."

"Judging by how impeccably she matched every *other* feature of your body," Clover said. "You must have left quite an impression from your previous performance."

"And judging by how much effort she put into reproducing every vein and bulge of your tool," Tara nodded. "I imagine she's had plenty of time to test if everything *works* correctly, as well."

"Well," Jessop grinned while he soaked up every inch of the girl's hourglass figure. "If she needs me to stand in as her model to *finish* the masterpiece, I'm ready whenever she needs me."

While everybody gaped at the girl's sexy body, she turned toward the front of the form, caressing her fingers over Jessop's doppelgänger face, then she leaned in to kiss his mouth, sliding her tongue sensuously over the curvature of his lips.

"Jesus," Jessop groaned, shifting his hips uncomfortably next to Clover and Gisella. "I must be just as hard as that statue right now–"

"So it would seem," Gisella nodded, grabbing the shaft of his dick with her right hand and squeezing it tightly. "Maybe even harder than it was *last night* when it was sliding between Tara's and my lips."

"There's something about watching her touching my body from a distance that's an incredible turn-on," Jessop said, rocking his hips against the old lady's hand.

"Even if it's not actually you in the *flesh*?" Clover laughed, noticing a small drop of dew slip out the tip of his tool.

"That's what makes it all the more erotic," Jessop nodded, groaning while he humped his dick into Gisella's hand.

The girl on the stage slowly slid her hand down the front of Jessop's carved chest, pausing just above the base of its upturned dick. Then she rolled her hand over the front of it, cupping her palm over its tightened testicles, sliding her tongue over her parted lips while she peered at the motionless figure. When she started sliding her fingers teasingly up the shaft of the phallus, Jessop moaned audibly, and she glanced toward his position on the front steps, winking at him softly.

"Oh my God," he panted as large streams of precum began to slide down the sides of his flapping organ. "I'm going to come soon if she keeps teasing me like that."

"I hope not," Gisella said, retracting her hand from Jessop's organ and slapping the side of his thigh. "You better make this last as long as you can. We're just getting started, and we intend to enjoy this performance along with the rest of the crowd until everybody's ready for the climax."

"Unghh," Jessop huffed, waving his thighs in and out while his dripping dick bobbed excitedly between his legs.

When the girl kneeled down in front of the figure's crossed legs and lowered her face onto the tip of its big prick, Jessop clenched his hands tightly by his side, trying to resist the temptation to grasp his throbbing hard-on and release his rapidly escalating sexual tension.

Gisella noticed his dick bouncing rapidly, and she reached out to pinch the tip of his swelling crown tightly with two fingers.

"Don't even *think* about it," she said, glancing at Jessop with angled eyebrows. "You can wait along with the rest of us until she's good and ready."

"But she's *killing* me," Jessop groaned while he stared at the girl's upturned ass as she lowered her head further down over the statue's upturned phallus.

"Think about dead cats if that helps you keep your mind focused," Clover chuckled, watching his dick twitching like it had a mind of its own.

"I'm thinking of a *different* kind of pussy right now," Jessop grunted while he ogled the girl's glistening vulva as she bent over further.

"Don't ruin it for her," Tara said from Jessop's opposite side. "Something tells me she's going to want to watch you when she finally decides to mount your dick."

"I can't wait," Jessop nodded as he rocked his hips into thin air. "I think I want to see that even more than she does."

"I wouldn't be so sure of that," Clover said, watching the girl raise her head off the statue's erection and straddle her feet on opposite sides of its hips as she slowly lowered her pussy toward the glistening shaft with her back toward the audience.

When she slipped the gleaming helmet into her folds and pressed her body downward, Jessop wasn't the only person groaning in rapture.

"Holy fuck, that's hot," Clover shuddered as she slipped two fingers into her hole.

"Who knew that fucking an inanimate object could be so arousing?" Tara nodded, pinching her nipples with one hand while she circled her clit with the other.

"Well, it *is* a pretty impressive bust," Gisella grunted, sliding her fingers over the crease of her dripping labia while she stared at the girl humping the wooden dick while she kissed Jessop's avatar face.

"The *cock*, or that girl's insane ass?" Jessop moaned while Gisella pinched the tip of his dick to keep him from shooting off.

"Both," Gisella nodded, slipping one finger into her pussy while she rolled her thumb over Jessop's dripping crown. "I'd be happy to fuck either *one* of them right now."

"This is driving me *crazy*," Jessop shuddered, clasping his knees together in an attempt to control the burgeoning pressure between his legs. "When is she going to turn around and let me see the rest of her body while she fucks me like I'm not even here?"

"She seems to be reading your mind," Clover said as the girl lifted her body off the statue's dripping phallus and turned around to face the crowd.

By now, the front of her body was completely coated in her own juices as the upturned erection of the statue gleamed in the flickering light of the candles surrounding the stage. Her chest was flushed in excitement and the nipples of her breasts darted like forty-five caliber bullets in the moving shadows. While she paused standing erect over the statue's organ, dripping her juices over its glistening head, you could hear a pin drop in the amphitheater while the rest of the crowd eagerly awaited the completion of her final act.

"Yes, please..." Jessop murmured as his own dick streamed rivers of precum down the sides of his throbbing shaft.

The girl lifted her head and locked eyes on Jessop, then she slowly lowered her body over the front of the statue, pausing with the parted lips of her pussy poised inches above the gleaming pole. When she pressed it gently inside her slit and crouched down lower to press it all the way inside her throbbing hole, everyone in the audience groaned as they caressed their own private parts, mimicking the movement of the girl on the stage while the entire grandstand rocked in unison.

"Now?" Jessop groaned while he peered at Gisella, begging her to allow him to touch his throbbing dick. "Can I touch my dick now?"

"Not yet," she smiled, squeezing his glans harder. "The moment you do, you'll just pop off. Enjoy the buildup a little longer until the girl is ready to come with you. It will make your climax all the more powerful."

"You better stand back when I finally let it go," Jessop grunted as his face reddened in rising frustration. "Because when I come *this* time, I'm going to shoot a mile into the air."

"I'm looking forward to it," Gisella smiled as she thrust two fingers in and out of her hole while she trilled her clit with her thumb.

As the girl on the stage stared directly at Jessop, her mouth began to gape open while she rocked her hips faster over the statue's hard phallus. When she placed her hand over her dripping mound and began to massage her cherry at the same time, she nodded toward him, as if giving him the signal to touch himself.

"Now?" Jessop said, peering at Gisella.

"Now," the old lady nodded. "I think *everybody's* ready now."

Jessop quickly grasped his hard-on with two hands and pumped it up and down as he squeezed it harder, groaning louder than anyone else in the stands. Then he tilted his hips upward while gripping his dick like his life depended on it, and he shot a series of giant strings high over his head, splattering over the heads and naked bodies of the surrounding spectators as they shuddered and moaned along with him. When the girl on the stage saw him spurting his load, she yawned her mouth open as a deep flush rolled over her tits, and she clasped her legs tightly closed while she jerked her body in rhythmic spasms, gushing her juices over the statue's balls and carved buttock cheeks.

The fountain of jets coming out of Jessop's dick seemed to go on forever while his friends trembled and quivered next to him, oblivious to the mess he was making as he coated their bodies with his shooting spunk. When he finally finished shaking and pulsing, he slumped forward together with the girl on the stage while they grinned at one another, nodding softly. He knew immediately what his next conquest would be, and he had no intention of letting the pretty native girl use his dormant avatar for her amusement any longer. From now on, he smiled, she wouldn't need to be left to her own devices to stimulate herself and wonder what it felt like to squeeze a real, throbbing hard-on.

7

———

"Well," Jessop said to Gisella after recovering from his powerful orgasm. "Since the girl on the stage obviously wants to make love to me, do I have your permission to meet with her *privately*?"

"Not yet," the old lady smiled, glancing up at the moonlit sky. "We need to wait until the moon is *full* to see who this month's winner are. We wouldn't want to compromise our performers' plans before they've had a chance to hookup with their designated partner on the stage."

"Even if I might open her eyes to a whole new world of possibilities? If she were chosen as one of the winners, perhaps my experience would allow her to be more creative and entertaining in her couple's demonstration..."

"You might have more practical experience hooking up with other partners," Gisella nodded. "But you haven't had the advantage of watching thousands of individual performances on this stage. I dare say that our young people's imaginations have already been broadened more than you could imagine."

"You might be right about that," Jessop grinned, wiping

the residue of leftover cum from the tip of his dripping dick against the inside of his thigh. "If these first three weeks are any sign of the limitless possibilities for both solo and paired combinations, I expect we've still got a lot to learn about how we can pleasure ourselves and our partners."

"Exactly," the old lady said, squeezing Jessop's balls playfully. "But keep practicing. You never know which one of you might have a chance to demonstrate your skills for the benefit of the whole tribe."

"Oh, we plan on *practicing*, alright," Jessop grinned, glancing at his two friends as they wiped his errant syrup off the sides of their bodies. "I'm pretty sure each of us will be ready when the time comes for us to show our stuff."

Having depleted their sexual energy watching the sexy native girl fucking the statue on the stage, the three friends slept like babies that night. While each of them dreamed of stranger ways to hookup with the natives on the stage, by the time they awoke, they were already charged up for the next performance scheduled for later in the evening.

"Holy crap!" Jessop gasped, waking up in a cold sweat. "I just had the craziest dream. I dreamt I was attacked by a swarm of flowers that were probing me and stroking me all over my body. It was alternately stimulating and terrifying at the same time."

"Maybe you were channeling your little experiment with the bees," Clover chuckled. "Or with the hungry pitcher plants, who were angry at you for stealing all the bees' attention."

"I had a sexy dream of my own," Tara nodded. "I dreamt I was sleeping peacefully in a grassy field when a giant snake slithered up beside me and started rubbing itself over my skin. Before long, it was curling up around me and squeezing my tits while it probed my pussy with its tail."

"Did you *enjoy* it?" Clover said, raising an eyebrow at Tara.

"I must have," Tara said, dragging her hand between her legs. "I haven't woken up this wet in a long time."

"Well, I had one too," Clover laughed. "I dreamt that I was a mythical hydra, but instead of slithering snakes on my head, I had big squirming *penises* for hair, who would mock anyone who passed by, telling them how they wanted to fuck them with their talking heads."

"I think you win the contest for weirdest dream," Tara nodded as she swept a loose strand of hair away from the side of Clover's face.

"It must be from all these all these erotic performances we see every night on the stage of the amphitheater," Clover said. "I don't know where these young tribespeople get all their crazy ideas. They've already *doubled* my catalog of positions and sex aids, and I haven't even been here one month."

"Maybe we should stay a little longer," Jessop chuckled. "It looks like after the full moon, we'll have free rein to mingle with the natives any way we please. I've had my eye on more than one that I'd like to hook up with as soon as the restrictions are lifted–"

"With girls or boys?" Tara said. "Because you seem to have enjoyed yourself pretty equally with both types of performers."

"A few of each, actually," Jessop grinned. "And not necessarily one at a time–"

"Well, you'll have a chance to pick up a few extra tips from tonight's presentation," Clover said. "It's going to be another *boy* this time, and I'm already getting turned on thinking about how he's going to wet his tool."

"If you're looking for new ways to *wet a tool,*" Jessop said as his hardening dick began to tent the bed cover upwards. "I'm more than happy to volunteer my services to help you stretch your imagination."

"Same here," Tara grunted, reaching under the bedspread to fondle Jessop's throbbing organ. "All those dreams about snakes have got me super horny and in need of some serious fucking."

"Are you interested in one cock or *two*?" Clover said, reaching over to her satchel to retrieve her magic balls. "Because I could use a bit more practice of my own before revealing my little secret to the rest of these tribespeople..."

L ater that evening, the trio returned to their customary position on the front steps of the amphitheater beside Gisella as she eyed their glistening and tumescent bodies with envy.

"You guys have a little advantage over the rest of us while we wait for the next erotic performance," she said. "There's three of you in your cabin every night, and you can hook up in all manner of configurations to test your sexual preferences any way you want..."

"That may be true," Clover smiled. "But maybe being alone with your fantasies and imagination before you have a chance to partner with someone else stimulates even *greater* ideas for enjoying the sexual experience."

"Judging by the new *prop* on the stage," Tara nodded as she squinted at a hollow wheel sitting at waist height in the middle of the platform. "I'm guessing we're going to see another one tonight."

While the drummer began to pound his drum to invite the next performer to the stage, the shadow of a naked youth began moving toward the rear of the dais. When he walked out onto the platform, he cupped his hands together over the front of his genitals, nodding as the audience applauded politely.

"I wish he'd show us his *cock*," Tara said, parting her legs slowly as she peered at the boy's sinewy body.

"It looks like he's hiding something in his hands," Clover nodded, squinting at his trembling fingers.

"I can't imagine what he's going to do with that *wheel*," Jessop said, wrinkling his forehead in curiosity.

The wheel was about a foot and a half in diameter and roughly two inches wide, made out of twisted bamboo with tall wooden spokes connecting the outer perimeter with a narrow, internal hub. The hub seemed to be lined with some kind of textured coating and a piece of what looked like cheese resting in the hollow middle. But when the boy lifted his arms and unfolded his hands, a surprised murmur spread around the amphitheater when the audience saw a small mouse scurrying in his palm.

"What the hell is he going to do with *that*?" Jessop said, leaning forward in confusion.

"I don't know," Tara said, furrowing her brow. "But I hope it's not going to be anything like my dream last night. Because that mouse doesn't belong anywhere other than the field, chewing on *cabbage*."

"It looks like he has other plans for the little rodent tonight," Clover said, watching the youth open a little door on his side of the wheel and placing the mouse inside the hollow cavity.

The mouse waddled unsteadily over the outer spines of the wheel, causing it to shake and wobble back and forth a few times, then the boy reached into the hollow inner hub, pulling out the small piece of cheese and carefully placing it on a hook positioned halfway up the inside of the wheel. When the mouse saw the piece of cheese, he immediately turned toward it and began running faster along the inner tread of the wheel, causing it to spin at a much faster and more consistent speed.

"Is that what I *think* it is?" Tara said, squinting her eyes in shock.

"If you mean his own vibrating *cock ring*, then I'd have to say yes," Clover chuckled as a big smile spread over her lips.

"That's ingenious," Jessop grinned as his flaccid organ immediately started to thicken and rise in tandem with the boy's on the stage.

"It seems to be working already," Clover nodded as she squeezed her thighs together, becoming increasingly aroused by the unique apparatus the youth had designed.

"Yes," Tara said, flaring her eyes as the boy's dick slowly began to expand and point toward the spinning hub of the wheel. "I can see all of his *cock* now."

"And it's fucking gorgeous," Clover panted while she spread her thighs apart and jilled her clit softly with two fingers.

"Do you think he'll be able to *fit* into that thing?" Jessop said, staring at the spinning inner circle.

The boy paused for a moment, then he inserted the tip of his erect organ in the front of the rotating hub, moaning in pleasure. Then he pressed his hips forward, thrusting his dick all the way through the gap until his glistening crown popped out the other side.

"Does *that* answer your question?" Clover groaned as she stuck two fingers into her sopping tunnel.

"Oh my God," Tara shuddered, rocking her hips softly next to Gisella. "Look at his beautiful, glistening manhood. He seems to have primed the inner surface with lube–"

"And it also seems to be coated with some kind of raised *nubs*," Jessop said, stroking his hard-on while he watched the youth rocking his hips back and forth as the mouse on the inside of the wheel continued to futilely chase the cheese pinned to the inner channel.

"It looks like a French tickler," Clover nodded. "That rubber that grows on your trees here can be fashioned for all *manner* of exotic purposes."

"Indeed it can," Gisella smiled, curling the tip of two fingers into the front of her dripping slit to massage her G-spot. "I've made a few of those for my *own* private pleasure more than once."

"Who needs *batteries* when you've got your own inexhaustible supply of energy running around your fields at any given time?" Clover chuckled, licking her lips as she watched the youth's glans reddening and swelling while the oscillating wheel stimulated his shaft and the base of his balls from the other side.

"Fuck me," Tara panted, jilling her clit harder while she gawked at the boy's thick pole popping in and out of the forward end of the spinning hub. "I sure wish that was my *pussy* he was fucking right now instead of that artificial piece of rubber."

"Yeah, but can your pussy stimulate him the way that *mouse* can?" Jessop said, twisting his fingers over the tip of his dripping glans, trying to mimic the action of the spinning wheel.

"Maybe not," grunted Tara. "But I could sure as hell give

him something softer and sweeter to hold onto while he was plowing my cavity."

"I'm not sure he needs anything else at this particular moment," Clover said, watching the boy's face redden and his mouth beginning to gape open as he pushed his dick all the way through the spinning hole and held his tightening balls against the flapping entrance while long strings of precum dripped from his swelling glans. "Something tells me that mouse is giving him all the stimulation he wants right now."

Suddenly, the youth threw his head back and placed his hands behind his neck as he tensed his legs and started spurting thick ropes of cum all over the stage in front of the oscillating wheel. When Jessop saw the boy climaxing, he couldn't help jetting his own spunk out of his throbbing organ, with the women following suit shortly after. When the boy finally finished shaking over the stage, he slowly retracted his organ from the still-spinning wheel, then he reached into the inner chamber to unhook the chunk of dangling cheese, handing it to the exhausted mouse, who gobbled it down greedily. When the wheel finally came to a rest, the audience immediately stood up and cheered the youth loudly, impressed with his creativity and erotic demonstration.

"That's something you don't see every day," Clover chuckled, wiping her slippery hands over the top of her thighs as she nodded at the spent youth.

"It looks like it's back to the drawing board to come up with more ideas for our next performance," Tara nodded.

"Or back to our *dreams*," Jessop grinned. "At least there, we're unrestricted conjuring up the craziest and wildest ideas."

8

Later that evening, the three friends went back to their cabin to discuss ideas for Clover's upcoming solo performance on the stage. With her turn only two days away, they wanted to maximize her chance of being chosen one of the winners for the couple's demonstration. As much as Tara would have liked to be one of the females selected for the paired performance, she knew that Clover's hidden secret would make her the crowd favorite. Plus, with both male and female parts after her transformation, the possibilities for hooking up with the chosen male would be all the more interesting.

"That was pretty fucking crazy," Tara said, squeezing Clover's ass cheeks when the trio fell into their oversize bed.

"Yeah," Clover said as she threaded her knee between Tara's dripping thighs. "These native people keep coming up with wilder and more innovative ways to stimulate themselves every night."

"Have you thought any more about you will do when it's your turn to go on the stage?" Tara said. "I assume you'll be using the magic balls to transform into a ladyboy to maximize the shock factor–"

"I've got a few ideas," Clover nodded. "But my choices are a bit limited without a partner to play with. As much as I think the audience will find my shemale imitation entertaining, I suspect they'll tire pretty quickly, watching me simply stroke my cock until I come."

"You could add some self-*sucking* like I did when I was up there alone," Tara said while she nibbled on Clover's nipples.

"Been there, done that," Clover said, running her fingers through Tara's hair. "We need something new to bring in another *wow* factor."

"Like a prop of some kind?"

"Yes, I'm just not sure what type. After the waterfall, the rocking horse, and the life-size carved statue, anything else seems kind of anticlimactic, if you'll forgive the pun."

"What if you created some kind of sex doll like that boy did with his gay lover mold?" Jessop said while he rubbed his cock against Clover's and Tara's asses. "Except in your case, you could make a female version, with tits and a pussy."

"I wouldn't know where to start," Clover said. "It probably takes weeks to shape the mold, let alone allowing time for the rubber to cure. We just don't have the skills to make something like that in the short time we have left."

"There's got to be *something* interesting you can do," Tara said, scrunching her forehead. "With all those extra parts to work with, it would be a shame not to use them all..."

"Maybe I could fuck myself up the ass with my cock," Clover laughed. "The audience seemed to like it when that native boy did it with his latex boyfriend."

"That would be a first," Tara chuckled. "But maybe not

the most exciting thing to watch a sexy ladyboy do, plus I can't imagine it would be very comfortable."

Clover paused for a moment as she exhaled heavily.

"Maybe I'll get some more ideas from the next performer," she said. "There's still one left to go before it's my turn to take the stage."

"Yeah, but the next one will be a *girl*, and you'll be in your *boy* disguise when you go up there."

"Not necessarily right away," Clover smiled. "I was planning on giving them a little taste of my *pussy* before I grow my boy cock and find a way to put that to better use–"

"Well, if you need a way to put it to better use right *now*," Tara grinned as she stuck two fingers inside Clover's wet hole. "I've got a few ideas that could be highly entertaining..."

T he following day, the trio joined Gisella on the front steps of the amphitheater as they rubbed their hands together in excitement.

"Are you almost ready for your turn in the spotlight?" the old lady asked Clover, squeezing the top of her thigh as she wriggled their hips together.

"I think so," Clover said with a lopsided smile. "I'm a bit nervous, though. I haven't been able to come up with any new ideas for stimulating myself that haven't already been tried."

"If you're planning on using those magic crystals to transform into a *shemale*, that might be enough all by itself. I'm sure the crowd would be thrilled to see a live cock on a pretty girl like yourself. That's something they've never witnessed before."

"Maybe," Clover frowned. "I just want to give them the sexiest show that I can. Plus, I was really hoping to be chosen as one of the two winners to participate in the final couple's demonstration in three nights' time."

"Well," Gisella chuckled. "Since you'll be performing as half woman and half *man*, your chances are twice as good. You could just as easily be chosen the *boy* winner as the girl winner."

"Hmm," Clover said, raising one eyebrow. "I never thought of it that way. I always assumed I'd have a *girl* for a partner if I went up there with a cock instead of a pussy. But I suppose it could work either way."

"Don't worry about any of that right now," Gisella said, turning toward the stage as the drummer began to pound his drum. "Just enjoy the show and rest up for tomorrow night."

As the beat began to escalate in pitch and frequency, Clover glanced at the stage, noticing a small object in the middle of the platform, concealed with a cloth cover.

"I guess she won't be using a life-size statue to stimulate herself this time," she chuckled out loud.

"Apparently not," Gisella nodded. "But as the saying goes, bigger isn't always better when it comes to sex. Especially *solo* sex."

When the drummer reached his crescendo and pounded the drum with one final, emphatic thump, another naked tribal girl slowly ascended the steps at the rear of the stage, walking toward the middle of the dais as the surrounding candles flickered over her petite frame. She was smaller and more slender than most of the other girls her age, with small breasts barely large enough to cast two short shadows over her chest. If it wasn't for her thick bush covering her mound and her firm buttock muscles that flexed as she bowed politely toward each side of the stage, she barely appeared old enough to reveal her naked figure, let alone fondle herself in full view of the entire tribe.

"Are you sure this one is *eighteen*?" Clover said, leaning over to whisper in Gisella's ear.

"Yes," the old lady nodded. "We keep meticulous records to make sure no one comes out before his or her appointed time. This one's just developed a little slower than the others."

"Well, she's certainly *beautiful* enough," Clover nodded, feeling her knees parting unconsciously as she soaked up the girl's pretty face and petite body.

With rosebud lips, a model-perfect nose, and brilliant emerald-green eyes, she looked like an exotic beauty plucked straight out of a Miss Universe pageant. And although her breasts were smaller than most girls her age, she made up for it with curves in all the other right places. With a narrow waist and swelling hips, her hourglass shape accentuated her femininity, drawing Clover's gaze down toward her softly bowed thighs and carved calf muscles.

"On second thought," Clover panted. "She seems plenty enough woman to me."

When the applause from the crowd died down, the girl paused for a moment, then she walked toward the concealed object on the stage and lifted the drape, throwing it softly behind her. The object was in the form of a woman's bust, cut off halfway up her torso, revealing her plump, half bosom, rounded shoulders and pretty face, complete with full, pouty, parted lips, and flowing hair falling softly onto the platform. The mold appeared to be made out of soft rubber again, and was tilted forty-five degrees upward, making the image of the rubber goddess look like she was peering upward at the sexy girl.

"Do you recognize that face?" Tara said to Clover, nudging her shoulder softly.

"On the *mold*, you mean?" Clover said. "No, but I think I recognize the *tits*..."

Although the bust's breasts were cut off at nipple height, they were roughly Clover's size and shape, and the nipples were colored bright pink to match her lighter skin tone.

"It looks like *Jessop's* not the only one who has a secret admirer here," Tara chuckled.

"Good to know," Clover laughed. "Although I'd have preferred if she didn't cut off my lower half."

The girl on the stage strutted a few paces in front of the mold, then she turned her body around as she shimmied her hips from side to side and bent her legs, slowly lowering her hips toward the mold's face. When her pussy was at face level, she parted her knees and pressed her groin against the bust's lips, grinding her pussy against its parted mouth.

"Mhhh," Clover grunted while she rocked her hips in synchronicity on the marble step of the amphitheater. "That's pretty fucking hot–"

"Are you *sure* you need your lower body right now?" Tara chuckled, watching Clover lick her lips while she ogled the sexy ass of the girl on the stage.

"Maybe not," Clover panted as small rivers of lubrication began to drip down the slit of her throbbing pussy. "I'd be happy to suck that pussy all day."

"So would *she*, it would appear," Tara nodded, pinching her nipples as she watched the performance.

The girl tilted her body forward a few degrees further, then she rested her knees on the floor beside the head of the bust. Then she placed her hands over the back of its head, pressing her vulva harder against the bust's glistening mouth. But what happened next surprised everyone, as a collective gasp echoed around the grandstand. A lifelike tongue suddenly pressed out of the rubber mold and began flapping over the girl's swelling nub while she leaned forward over the form, displaying her dripping wet pussy for everyone to see.

"Holy fuck!" Clover said, sitting up suddenly. "What the hell is that thing? It almost looks like a *real tongue*–"

"Maybe she cut a hole in the stage and someone stuck their head into the mask from below the platform," Tara said, squinting her eyes in shock.

"That's against the rules," Gisella said, shaking her head. "Everyone is instructed beforehand that the performance must be performed entirely solo."

"But with the aid of props?" Clover said.

"Yes, but only self-made ones."

"What's making the tongue *move* like that, then?" Clover asked.

"Maybe she stuck a snake under the mold," Jessop said, half-kidding. "And it's slithering in excitement from all the shaking of the form."

"Is that allowed?" Clover said, wrinkling her forehead at Gisella.

"Well, the last boy got away with using a *mouse*," she nodded. "And the pitcher plant was also organically powered..."

"Well, *whatever* it is," Clover said, opening her legs and rolling her fingers over her burning clit while she watched the animated bust licking the girl's pussy. "I wouldn't mind having one of those in my nightstand on lonely nights. That puts all of my other sex toys back home to shame."

But just when Clover and the rest of the crowd didn't think it could get any sexier, the girl on the stage pulled her hips away from the face of the rubber mold and turned around to face the audience, squatting over the upturned face of the bust while she pulled her knees apart on the floor of the platform. As she slid her hands up her belly toward her small breasts, she pinched both of her swollen nipples tightly, rolling them firmly between her fingers while she stared in Clover's direction.

"Fuck yes," Clover pantomimed back toward the girl as she rolled her tongue over the top of her lips. "Grind your pussy on my face. I want to drink your juices when you come."

As the animated tongue of the bust pressed a few inches further out of its parted lips, it slowly slithered down the parted crease of the girl's dripping vulva toward her puckering sphincter, bathing her starfish in her own juices before pushing two inches into her butthole. As her face flushed a deep shade of crimson, the girl tilted her head upward, rocking her hips harder against the shaking bust until she squirted six huge jets of liquid between her splayed legs, straight toward Clover.

When Clover saw the girl climaxing directly in front of her, she couldn't hold back her rising pleasure any longer, and she grunted loudly, gushing her own juices hard out between her parted legs, creating an arched fountain of mingling juices in the flickering candlelight, rivaling the display of the Bellagio Hotel in Las Vegas. When the two women finally stopped shaking and gushing onto the stage, the crowd paused in shock for a moment, then everyone stood up, giving a standing ovation to the girl as their dripping erections and wet bushes waved in front of their hips.

"Did that stimulate your creative juices again?" Gisella grinned, rubbing her hand softly over the insides of Clover's dripping thighs.

"It certainly did, in more ways that one," Clover panted

as she smiled back at the pretty girl on the stage. "I think I know exactly what I want to do now for my solo performance tomorrow night."

"I can't wait," the old lady said as she slid her hand over Clover's throbbing pussy while she fingered her flaring bulb. "And something tells me, neither can the rest of the crowd."

9

———

After the girl with the rubber face mold left the stage, Clover asked Gisella if she could speak with the girl privately. When she said yes, she followed her back to her cabin, knocking quietly on her door. The girl's eyes flew open when she saw Clover standing on her doorstep, but when Clover explained she only needed a few minutes of the girl's time, she invited her inside.

"I enjoyed your performance very much," Clover said, trying not to stare at the girl's still-dripping bush and inner thighs.

"Thank you," the girl smiled. "Watching you made it all the more pleasurable for me."

Clover glanced at the rubber mold the girl had brought back with her to her cabin, squinting at the gap in its lips where the strange tongue had been flapping out earlier.

"Is that mold fashioned after *me*?" she asked.

"Yes," the girl blushed. "I've been watching you in the grandstand these past few nights, and I think you're very sexy."

"That's very kind of you to say," Clover said. "I think you are, too. I haven't come that hard in a long time."

"Me neither," the girl said. "I imagine it would be even *more* intense if we were able to hook up for real."

"I know," Clover frowned. "But I've been told the young people are off limits until after the full moon. Something about saving themselves until the winners are announced."

"Yes," the girl said, staring at Clover's huge nipples. "So have we. It's a shame to have to wait when we're both so attracted to one another–"

"We might not have to wait too much longer," Clover smiled. "That's actually why I came to see you. You see, it's my turn to perform on the stage tomorrow night, and I wanted to ask you a favor..."

"By all means," the girl said. "Anything to help you raise your game."

"Well, I was wondering if you might be willing to let me use your little *prop*–"

"Won't that be a bit strange?" the girl said, pinching her eyebrows together. "Making love to your own *face*? Won't it be a bit redundant using the same prop two nights in a row?"

"I've got something else I'm planning to do to raise the stakes," Clover smiled. "I'm confident the audience will find my presentation sufficiently unique."

"Okay," the girl nodded. "I'll be happy to set it up for you beforehand if you wish."

"That would be very kind of you," Clover said, peering at the rubber mold. "I just had one other question before I decide to make this the centerpiece of my performance..."

"Of course," the girl said. "Ask away."

"Can you tell me how you got the tongue to move so realistically, and what is inside the mold? Because I might be delving a little *deeper* than you did when it's my turn to make love to it."

The girl hesitated for a moment, then she raised an eyebrow, peering at Clover with a playful grin.

"I can, but only if you promise not to tell anyone. I don't want to give away the secret until the final winners are announced. I believe the element of mystery will help to increase *both* of our chances at being chosen for the couple's presentation."

"Not to worry," Clover smiled. "My lips are sealed. At least my *real* ones. As for my pretty doppelgänger sitting on the floor over there, I can't make any promises..."

The next day, Tara and Jessop kept pestering Clover to disclose what she planned to do on the stage that night, asking her what she'd spoken to the pretty native girl about when she visited her cabin the previous night. But Clover refused to give away the secret, hoping the added mystery would only elevate their enjoyment of her performance that much more. When they heard the drummer begin his introduction of the next performance, they headed over to the amphitheater, with Clover holding back in the shadows behind the stage while her accomplice placed the rubber mold back on the stage with the cover.

When the drumbeat finally finished, she could feel her heart pounding in her chest, hoping everything would turn out the way she planned. As she clasped the mage's magic balls in her sweaty palm, she ascended the steps at the rear of the dais, nodding politely to the crowd while they acknowledged her arrival. Gisella had arranged for the pretty native girl who'd performed the previous night to join her and Clover's friends on the front steps of the theater, and Clover winked at her while she stood nervously in front of the concealed bust.

When she lifted the cover and tossed it to the side of the stage, she heard the disappointed murmurs of the crowd when they saw the same prop as the previous night. But Clover knew she had an ace up her sleeve, and she planned to have them eating out of her hand soon enough. But not until she teased them with a little sexy intro of her own. She turned around and shimmied her bare ass like the girl had done the night before, then she mimicked her technique, lowering her hips slowly until her pussy rested over the gaping mouth of the rubber bust. As she rocked her vulva over its parted lips, the strange tongue from inside the cavity began to press through the opening once again, flapping softly over her dripping labia.

Meanwhile, the group sitting on the front steps of the bandstand peered at one another with confused expressions, shaking their heads in dismay.

"Is this all she's planning to do tonight?" Gisella said to her friends with a wrinkled forehead.

"To be honest," Jessop nodded. "We're not entirely sure. She wouldn't tell *us* what she was going to do, either."

"I know she has at least *one* extra surprise planned," Tara said. "Give her a little longer before you judge prematurely. I'm pretty sure the rest of the audience will be more than satisfied before she's finished."

"I hope so," Gisella said, rubbing her thighs together as she remembered her sexy hookup with Clover a few nights ago.

While she humped her hips harder against the rubber face of the bust and the flapping tongue continued teasing her dripping pussy, Clover slowly began rubbing the magic balls together in her closed hand. With the front of her body turned away from the audience, they couldn't see her gland gradually growing and elevating over her hips. But as her slit began to meld together and her labia bunched into a tight ballsack nestled below her cheeks, their eyes suddenly flared open as they leaned forward, trying to understand exactly what was going on.

Clover paused for a few moments to add to the suspense, then she raised her ass a few inches over the bust and tilted her hips forward, displaying her thick ladyboy cock pointing straight downward. As the bust's tongue flapped upward toward her glistening crown, she pointed her tip into its mouth, slowly sinking her entire erection deep into its cavity. When she felt the warm, undulating tongue inside the mold begin to coil itself around her shaft and squeeze it tighter, she moaned loudly, pressing her balls hard against the gaping mouth of the mold.

She'd never felt anything massaging her tool like this before, and as she wrapped her arms around the back of the mold's head while groaning in delirious pleasure, she gaped her mouth open, savoring the delicious feeling of the writhing tongue squeezing and sucking her dick inside the instrument while its other end slithered down over her balls to tease her puckering butthole. She could have easily come this way, emptying her seed inside its convulsing belly, but she wanted the audience to see her coming in her full glory while they gawked at her big cock and sexy ladyboy figure.

Just as she reached the edge of climax, she pulled her throbbing dick out of the bust's mouth and turned around, displaying her bobbing erection flapping over her tight ball-sack for the entire crowd to see. Between alternate gasps and moans, they clapped and cheered wildly, jerking their hard-ons and jilling their sopping pussies while they stared at

Clover like she was from another planet. When she saw that everyone was sufficiently aroused by her demonstration, Clover glanced at Tara and Jessop nodding enthusiastically next to the old lady, then she peered at the petite native girl sitting next to them while she thrust the fingers of her right hand knuckle-deep in her dripping pussy as she stared at Clover's bouncing pole.

Clover could feel the pressure building up in her balls as she watched the girl and the rest of the naked natives stroking themselves, and she had no intention of keeping anyone waiting to longer than necessary. With her swelling dick pointing straight up over her belly, she squatted down over the front of the bust, then she positioned her starfish directly over its long, undulating tongue, sitting down over its face while the fleshy appendage sunk deep into her butt-hole. Clover found the experience more stimulating than she imagined, and as rivers of precum streamed out of her dripping crown and down the sides of her bobbing shaft, she didn't even have to touch herself to bring herself to the peak of her pleasure.

As her balls tightened into a vice-grip below the base of her throbbing erection, she felt her juice shooting up the length of her pole until it exploded out the top, gushing all over her bouncing tits and reddening face while she screamed at the top of her lungs, enjoying the longest and most powerful orgasm of her life. When she saw the pretty native girl on the front steps gushing her juices along with her, she grabbed her dick with both hands, feeling it pulsating in her hands while she milked every last drop of cum out of her balls. By the time she finished climaxing, she peered up and scanned the audience, whose hands had been so busy stimulating themselves at the same time, they scarcely had time to respond to her erotic performance.

But as an eerie hush fell over the amphitheater, everyone suddenly stood up and began clapping and cheering wildly, with loud shouts of "Bravo!", "Encore!", and "Viva la Diva!" emanating from every corner of the stadium. When the standing ovation finally subsided after a full two minutes, Gisella nodded as she turned toward Clover's two friends.

"Well, I guess we know who the *first* winner of this month's presentations is going to be," she smiled.

"Will she be representing the *women's* or the *men's* side of the equation for the couple's performance?" Tara said, lifting an eyebrow.

"Does it really matter?" the old lady said. 'Judging by the reaction of the crowd, it looks like they'll be happy to see her reprise her role either way."

"Well, I know at least *one* person who'd be happy to be her muse," Jessop chuckled, glancing at the petite native girl still shaking next to him as she clamped her hands tightly between her quivering legs while she stared at Clover with her mouth agape.

10

———

After Clover completed her solo performance on the stage, the three friends went back to their cabin, excited to see who would be voted the winners of the month's presentations. Gisella mentioned that voting would take place early the next day, with the winners announced in the afternoon, so everybody could prepare for the couple's demonstration. When Clover and Tara were announced as the two winners, they hugged each other excitedly, then they furrowed their foreheads, suddenly worried about what they'd do to meet the high expectations of the crowd.

"I don't know if I'm more excited or terrified," Tara said to Clover and Jessop when they returned to their cabin. "I'm happy that the two of us will be performing on stage, but I don't know what we can do that hasn't already been done before. I don't want to disappoint all the people who voted for us."

"Well," Clover smiled. "If I transform into a ladyboy again, they won't have seen someone fucking a real girl before–"

"Yes, but won't they be *expecting* that, now that they know who'll be joining up together? Besides, how many different ways can a boy fuck a girl that hasn't already been tried?"

"Or a *ladyboy*," Clover chuckled.

The three friends paused for a moment while they pondered the possibilities, then Jessop suddenly gasped, flaring his eyes open.

"What if you *both* turned into ladyboys?" he said. "Surely, they'll never have seen or contemplated something like that. The possibilities would be almost endless in that match-up."

"Hmm," Clover said, squinting her eyes toward Tara. "That could be pretty exciting. We haven't done anything like that since we left the Sannyan erotic temple."

"Yeah, but in that case, we were transformed into *hermaphrodites*, not ladyboys," Tara said. "In *this* case, we'll only have the male equipment to work with, so our connection opportunities are more limited."

"True," Clover frowned. "But we'll still have all our other girl parts, and that's half the appeal of watching ladyboys. The crowd can still enjoy our sexy female figures while fantasizing about what they'd like to do with our boy-cocks if they had their way with us."

"Okay," Tara said, feeling her juices dribbling down the inside of her thigh while she imagined all the ways she and Clover could have fun stimulating each other as two ladyboys. "But are we sure this is going to *work*? We don't even know if your magic crystals will work on somebody other than you–"

"There's only one way to find out," Clover smiled, reaching into her satchel to hand Tara the glowing crystals. "Let's practice for a bit before we try it on the stage."

After Clover and Tara discovered the magic crystals worked equally well on both of them, they experimented with different positions and stimulation techniques while Jessop looked on and gave them feedback, then they took notes of their performance plan, temporarily returning back to their girl forms. When the drumbeat started up later that night to announce the start of the full-moon performance, the three friends headed back toward the amphitheater, with Clover and Tara waiting behind the stage while Jessop took his customary position beside Gisella on the front-row seat.

"Are you ready for this?" Clover said to Tara, grasping her hand excitedly while the pace of the drumbeat sped up to a crescendo.

"I think so," Tara nodded. "Let's give them a show like they've never seen before."

"I'm way ahead of you, girl," Clover smiled, squeezing Tara's ass softly.

When the drumbeat finished and they walked up onto the stage hand-in-hand, they heard the murmurs of the audience, who were clearly disappointed Clover was appearing in her girl form instead of the expected ladyboy guise. But the two girls had carefully planned their performance, and they intended to warm up the audience with a little girl-on-girl action before ramping up their interaction for the climactic finish. After the audience finished applauding politely, Clover and Tara lay down beside one another on the soft sheepskin mats on the platform, rubbing their bodies together softly while interlacing their legs between each other's thighs.

After kissing each other passionately for a few minutes,

Clover pulled Tara's right leg upwards toward her shoulder, then she squatted overtop of her in a scissor position, grinding their pussies together while they moaned in each other's mouths. Clover heard the impatient murmurs of the crowd stop, and when she glanced out the corner of one eye, she noticed many of the men and women in the audience spreading their legs apart as they began to fondle their genitals.

"It looks like we've got their attention now," she whispered into Tara's ear, pulling her friend's other leg upward until both of her feet were pinned behind her head like Tara had done with her earlier solo performance.

Then she squatted in front of Tara's upturned hips and lowered her ass down on top of Tara's glistening pussy, joining their buttocks together like two rounded half-busts while they rubbed their dripping vulvas together. When the audience saw their labia stretched apart and their juices streaming down their shining slits, they moaned in pleasure, stroking and jilling themselves harder. But when Tara tilted her head toward their joined hips and began slurping their tribbing clits at the same time, a loud moan began to spread around the theater as the sound of a hundred shifting bodies on the hard stone steps echoed through the stadium.

"Okay," Clover whispered to Tara as she began rolling the magic crystals in her hand. "Now that we've got them properly warmed up, let's *really* give them something to talk about."

As Clover's ladyboy cock began to swell and push outward, she kept it hidden from the view of the audience with the tight connection of her ass resting over Tara's hips. When it reached its fully erect state, she raised her hips upward a few inches to display her bouncing instrument, then she placed the tip next to Tara's open mouth, thrusting her pole deep into her friend's throat.

"Ooohh," the audience gasped in unison, imagining what it would feel like to suck a ladyboy's cock. While they stroked their rock-hard erections and dripping pussies, they gawked at the two women's asses while Clover rammed her balls against Tara's chin.

The two friends had practiced this before in their cabin, so they were comfortable performing such an intimate act, and as Tara relaxed her throat, she groaned in pleasure while Clover rocked her tightening balls over her flaring clit.

"Are you ready for the next step in our devious plan?" Clover grunted into Tara's ear as she bent over her body, rubbing their tits together while Tara sucked her throbbing hard-on.

"Mm-hmm," Tara nodded as Clover passed her the magic crystals and Tara began to rub them together in her hand.

When Tara's boy-cock started to harden and swell between her legs, Clover pulled her hips backward a few inches to hide the second tool, rubbing her dripping erection over Tara's newly formed testicles to bring her to greater heights of ecstasy. With both of their cocks now hidden from view, they paused for a moment to heighten the suspense, then they separated their hips to show their combined organs, eliciting a loud gasp from the audience.

Clover shifted her hips forward a few inches and when her ass slid overtop Tara's bobbing erection, it slapped against the back of her ass while Tara rocked her hips upward, sliding her instrument between the crack of Clover's ass. As they continued humping their hips together, teasing the crowd with the possibility of Tara inserting her dick into Clover's anus, she pointed the tip over Clover's puckering rosebud. Suddenly, Clover flipped her body around to face the audience with her ass resting over Tara's belly while their two cocks pointed up next to each other.

With the audience pinching their eyebrows, wondering what the two ladyboys were going to do next, Clover reached out her hands and grabbed their cocks with both of her hands, squeezing them together while pumping her hands up and down their connected shafts. As the audience groaned even louder, the two women began rocking their hips while they frotted their dripping dicks together, moaning in unison with the appreciative crowd.

But when Clover saw the precum streaming out the tips of their cocks like a bubbling spring, she squeezed Tara's hips with her thighs and pinched the tips of their tools tightly to keep them both from popping off. As much as Clover would have loved to create a fountain of the two ladyboys spouting their cocks together for the entire crowd to see, she and Tara had planned one final act that the crowd had not anticipated. As she began to shift her hips backwards towards Tara's lowered head, she moved her face closer toward Tara's bouncing pole until both women had inhaled each other's instruments into their respective mouths.

"Unghh," the audience groaned even louder as they jerked and trilled their genitals faster, growing closer to climax along with the two women on the stage while Clover and Tara sucked each other's ladyboy cocks and squeezed their balls softly with their hands.

"Mmmm," the two girls moaned in their tight sixty-nine position, nodding to indicate they were both on the precipice of climaxing.

When they felt the shafts of their dicks beginning to pulse, they quickly lifted their heads off each other's erections, watching their spunk shoot out of their flexing hard-ons and spraying over their bouncing breasts and glistening lips while they extended their tongues, happily lapping down each other's ladyboy juices. While they were shooting their honey over each other's faces and bellies, Clover glanced up and noticed everyone in the audience shaking and squirting along with them–including Jessop and Gisella, who were busy humping each other in their laps.

"That should give them something to talk about for a while," Clover smiled, turning around to peer at Tara with a flushed face.

"Yeah," Tara panted. "I'm pretty sure they haven't seen anything like *this* before."

"Maybe we should stick around and do a little more cross-pollinating to pick up some extra ideas."

"I'm game if you are," Tara nodded.

"It looks like Jessop is too," Clover laughed, watching him squeeze Gisella's ass as he sucked on her nipples while they quivered in each other's laps.

*R*eady for more erotic chills and thrills? Read the next volume in Clover's Fantasy Adventures: The Magic Pool. *Buy direct and save at victoriarusherotica. Or download from your favorite online bookstore here: retailer links.*

This hot spring stimulates a lot more than just your muscles...

ALSO BY VICTORIA RUSH

Adult Fairytales:

The Enchanted Forest: An Erotic Fairytale

The Land of Giants: An Erotic Fairytale

The Dragon's Lair: An Erotic Fairytale

Witch's Brew: An Erotic Fairytale

The Mage's Spell: An Erotic Fairytale

The Mermaid Lagoon: An Erotic Fairytale

The Coven: An Erotic Fairytale

Rapunzel: An Erotic Fairytale

The Seven Dwarfs: An Erotic Fairytale

The Land of Mutants: An Erotic Fairytale

The Erotic Temple: A Sexy Fairytale (Coming Soon)

Erotica Themed Bundles:

Voyeur: Lesbian Erotica Bundle

Public Affairs: A Lesbian Anthology

Futa Fantasies: The Ladyboy Collection

Threesomes: The Lesbian Collection

Threesomes - Volume 2: The Lesbian Collection

First Time: A Lesbian Anthology

Hedonism: An Erotic Anthology

Switch Hitters: Bisexual Erotica

Taboo Erotica: The Lesbian Series

BDSM: The Lesbian Collection

Party Games: The Erotic Collection

Party Games 2: The Erotic Collection

All Girl 1: Lesbian Erotica Bundle

All Girl 2: Lesbian Erotica Bundle

All Girl 3: Lesbian Erotica Bundle

All Girl 4: Lesbian Erotica Bundle

Erotic Fairytale Bundles:

Clover's Fantasy Adventures: Books 1 - 5

Clover's Fantasy Adventures: Books 6 - 10

Erotic Fantasy:

Pirate's Bounty: A Time Travel Adventure

Wild West: A Time Travel Adventure

Private Riley: A Time Travel Adventure

Cleopatra's Secret: A Time Travel Adventure

Bounty Hunter 2125: A Time Travel Adventure

Ninja Assassin: A Time Travel Adventure

The 300: A Time Travel Adventure

Arabian Nights: An Erotic Fairytale (coming soon...)

Steamy Time Travel Bundles:

Riley's Time Travel Adventures: Books 1 - 5

Lesbian Erotica:

The Dinner Party: Lesbian Voyeur Erotica

The Darkroom: Bisexual Voyeur Erotica

Naked Yoga: Lesbian Transgender Erotica

Nude Cruise: Bisexual Voyeur Erotica

Rush Hour: Taboo Public Sex

The Girl Next Door: First Time Lesbian Erotic Romance

Girls' Camp: Lesbian Group Sex

Wet Dream: Ladyboy Fantasy Erotica

The Convent: Taboo Sex with a Nun

Sex Robot: A Dream Sex Machine

The Personal Trainer: Getting Pumped at the Gym

The Dominatrix: BDSM Lesbian Domination

Webcam Chat: Lesbian Online Sex

Paint Me: A Kinky Bodypainting Workshop

The Toy Party: Girls Sharing Sex Toys

The Costume Party: Strapping One On

Swedish Sauna: Lesbian Group Sex

The Therapist: Taboo Lesbian Erotica

Elevator Shaft: Bisexual Threesomes Erotica

Ladyboy: Lesbian Transgender Erotica

Peep Show: Lesbian Voyeur Erotica

The Dare: Public Sex Erotica

Maid Service: Lesbian Threesomes Erotica

The Hitchhiker: First Time Lesbian Erotica

The Housesitter: Spycam Lesbian Erotica

The Spa: Lesbian Group Orgy

Parlor Games: Blindfold Sex Party

The Exchange Student: First Time Lesbian Erotica

The Hostel: Bisexual Group Erotica

The Harem: Lesbian Erotic Romance

The Orient Express: Lesbian Voyeur Erotica

The First Lady: A Forbidden Lesbian Erotic Romance

The Slave: Lesbian BDSM Erotica

The Masseuse: Lesbian Sensuous Erotica

Too Close for Comfort: Lesbian Forbidden Erotica

Naked Twister: A Wild Party Game

Lexi: The Sex App (Lesbian Fantasy Erotica)

Call Girl: Lesbian Bisexual Threesomes Erotica

Circle Jill: Lesbian Masturbation Workshop

The Viewing Room: Masturbation Voyeur Erotica

Spin the Bottle: A Kinky Party Game

The Hair Salon: Lesbian Voyeur Erotica

Tribadism 1: Girls Only Sex Workshop

Tribadism 2: The Art of Scissoring

Tribadism 3: Threeway Hookups

The Kiss: A Game of Oral Sex

Pledge Week: Sorority Sisters

Carny Games 1: A Wild Sex Party

Carny Games 2: A Kinky Sex Party

Carny Games 3: An Erotic Sex Party

Dreamscape: An Artificial Reality Game

Glory Hole: Guess Who's On the Other Side

Joy Ride: A Late Night Erotic Bus Trip

The Blind Girl: An Erotic Romance(Coming Soon)

Lesbian Erotica Bundles:

Jade's Erotic Adventures: Books 1 - 5

Jade's Erotic Adventures: Books 6 - 10

Jade's Erotic Adventures: Books 11 - 15

Jade's Erotic Adventures: Books 16 - 20

Jade's Erotic Adventures: Books 21 - 25

Jade's Erotic Adventures: Books 26 - 30

Jade's Erotic Adventures: Books 31 - 35

Jade's Erotic Adventures: Books 36 - 40

Jade's Erotic Adventures: Books 41 - 45

Jade's Erotic Adventures: Books 46 - 50

Fifty Shades of Jade: Superbundle

Standalone Stories:

The Polynesian Girl: A Lesbian Erotic Romance